# Paula's Patches

Gabriella Aldeman

Illustrated by

Rocío Arreola Mendoza

free spirit
PUBLISHING®

**Library of Congress Cataloging-in-Publication Data**
Names: Aldeman, Gabriella, author. | Arreola Mendoza, Rocío, illustrator.
Title: Paula's patches / Gabriella Aldeman ; illustrated by Rocío Arreola Mendoza.
Description: Minneapolis, MN : Free Spirit Publishing, an imprint of Teacher Created Materials, Inc., 2023. | Audience: Ages 5–9.
Identifiers: LCCN 2022053275 (print) | LCCN 2022053276 (ebook) | ISBN 9781631987335 (hardcover) | ISBN 9781631987342 (ebook) | ISBN 9781631987359 (epub)
Subjects: CYAC: Repairing—Fiction. | Pants—Fiction. | BISAC: JUVENILE FICTION / Social Themes / Self-Esteem & Self-Reliance | JUVENILE FICTION / Social Themes / Poverty & Homelessness | LCGFT: Picture books.
Classification: LCC PZ7.1.A43444 Pau 2023  (print) | LCC PZ7.1.A43444  (ebook) | DDC [E]—dc23
LC record available at https://lccn.loc.gov/2022053275
LC ebook record available at https://lccn.loc.gov/2022053276

Free Spirit Publishing does not have control over or assume responsibility for author or third-party websites and their content. Parents, teachers, and other adults: We strongly urge you to monitor children's use of the internet.

Edited by Marjorie Lisovskis
Cover and interior design by Courtenay Fletcher

Printed in China

**Free Spirit Publishing**
An imprint of Teacher Created Materials
9850 51st Avenue North, Suite 100
Minneapolis, MN 55442
(612) 338-2068
help4kids@freespirit.com
freespirit.com

FSC
www.fsc.org
MIX
Paper | Supporting
responsible forestry
FSC® C144853

To my daughter, Lucia. Your determination and boundless creativity inspire me every day.
—G.A.

∧ ∧ ∧ ∨ ∧ ∨ ∨ ∧ ∨ ∨

For you, little child full of curiosity and creativity, may adversity never stop you, and may your ideas make this world a kinder and better place. I can't wait to see the future you create!
—R.A.M.

# Rrrip!

I froze at the sound
of my pants tearing.

"Uh-oh," said George. "Can you get new ones, Paula?"

"Maybe," I murmured. But I knew I would have to wait for the next batch of hand-me-downs from my cousin.

"Shh, please don't tell," I pleaded.

I didn't want anyone else to notice the hole. My teacher would try to help and all the kids would laugh at me.

"I won't," promised George.

At my desk, I covered my leg with my right hand and tried writing with the left. The P's came out particularly wriggly.

"Is your hand all right, Paula?" asked Zoila.

"It just needs a rest."

I looked down and noticed the name on Zoila's backpack: "Penelope." I guess Zoila got hand-me-downs too.

At lunch, I placed the food tray on my lap to hide the tear.

"Do you need space for your tray, Paula?" asked Libby.

# SPLAT!

"Oh no," cried Libby. "My lunch bag ripped! George, watch out for the milk!"

Startled, George toppled backward. An avalanche of spaghetti poured all over his favorite soccer shirt.

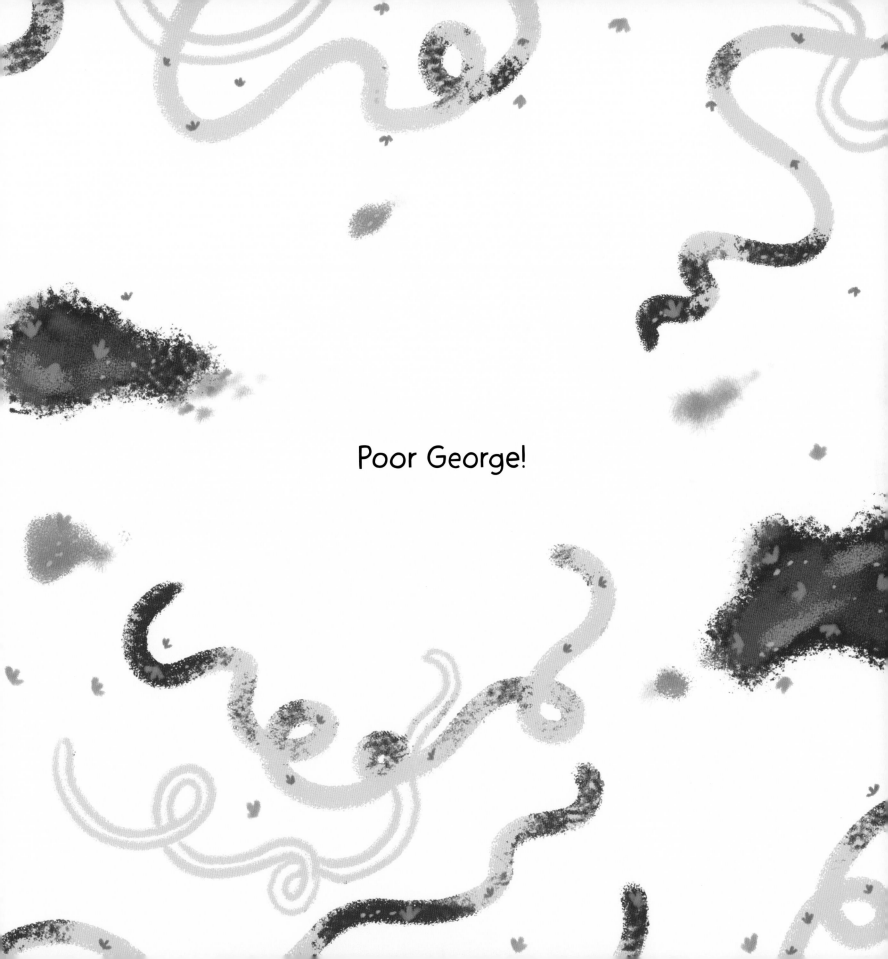

Poor George!

At recess, I tied my sweater around my waist like an apron.

"I am Paula the Powerful, Protector of the Playground! George, you are Sir Soccer, the Swiftest Striker in All the World!"

"See?" I said. "You already have the round symbol—just like a superhero!"

George seemed to feel better.

I didn't.

On the bus ride home,
Libby sat next to me.
I used my sweater to
cover the hole.

"It's like a blanket,"
I explained. "I got cold."

"I love blankets," said Libby. "My mom and I sewed this quilt using my old baby clothes. We cut out patches of fabric and stitched them together."

"You made this from old stuff? It's so pretty!"

Libby nodded. And I got an idea.

At home, I dashed to the closet. Mami
kept old, worn clothes and fabric scraps
in a bin at the back.

There were rainbows and smiley faces, stripes and polka dots, penguins and superheroes. And soccer balls. For George!

There was enough fabric to make patches for everyone in class. I would ask Mami for help.

The next day at circle time, I presented the gifts.

"I made these patches. You can each pick your favorite."

Some kids stared. My tummy flip-flopped. Then I heard Zoila murmur, "Patches?"

What was I thinking? My classmates didn't want my homemade patches. They could probably go to the store and buy new things.

But what about George's spaghetti stain? Or Zoila's backpack?

I took a deep breath and started again. "These patches are like stickers for jackets or bags. Or bandages to cover tears or stains."

I waited a moment.

Then Zoila reached out and grabbed a large patch from the pile.
"I can use this to cover my sister's name on my backpack."

One by one, my classmates picked
out their favorite patches.

"Can I sew this to a teddy?
Mine has a hole."

"My jacket will look
brand new!"

Now we all had patches—for mending, and decorating, and making things our very own.

Everyone was smiling . . .

. . . and guess who had the **BIGGEST** grin of all!

# A Note from the Author

My daughter's pants used to tear all the time. This resulted in big feelings—mostly from me. When I was a child, I got teased about my clothes and the way they fit.

One time, at a birthday party, my jeans got caught on the edge of a slide and tore as I went down. The hole was so big it exposed my bottom! I probably should have told a grown-up. Instead, I spent the rest of the party sitting down, pretending I had a tummy ache. I even missed out on singing happy birthday and eating cake. I wish I'd had a jacket to tie around my waist. More than anything, I wish I had realized that it was okay. And not my fault.

If you've ever felt like Paula or me because your clothes are torn or old, or don't fit quite right, please know you are not alone.

Remember how Zoila asks Paula if her hand is all right? And Libby asks Paula whether she needs space for her lunch tray? If you spot a classmate feeling low, ask them if they are okay. They might not always tell you the whole story. But your kindness may be the encouragement they need to feel better or come up with their own creative solution.

Paula's solution to her worries is to make colorful patches for her friends and for herself. You too can create patches like Paula's—or come up with new designs of your own. On this page and the next are some ideas for you to try. Use your imagination, and have fun!

## Fun with Fabric

### Paula's Patches

Use fabric to make patches like Paula's.

**What you need**

* scissors
* scrap of fabric
* glue or clear nail polish
* embroidery thread (optional)
* safety pins

**What you do**

1. Cut out any shape from a piece of fabric.

2. Apply a layer of glue or nail polish around the edges to prevent fraying. Let it dry.

3. Optional: If you wish, use embroidery thread to make decorative stitches around the edge of the patch.

4. Add a safety pin or two and pin your patch to decorate a jacket or bag. Or ask an adult to sew your creation to cover a tear or stain.

## Paula's Bookmarks

Make your own bookmark with leftover fabric scraps. Happy reading!

### What you need

* thin cardboard (such as from a cereal box)
* glue
* scraps of fabric
* scissors

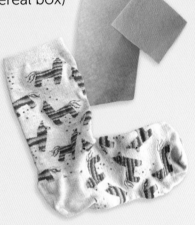

### What you do

1. Draw a rectangle on the cardboard and cut it out.
2. Spread a thin layer of glue over one side of the cardboard.
3. Place your fabric (one or more pieces) over the side covered in glue. Let it dry.
4. Use scissors to trim off any excess fabric.
5. Repeat steps 2 to 4 on the other side of the cardboard.

## Paula's Pouches

Did you know you can make a drawstring pouch with fabric and string? No sewing required! You can use it to store your favorite treasures.

### What you need

* round object, such as a plate
* pen or marker
* 12" × 12" fabric
* scissors
* hole puncher (optional)
* string or ribbon

### What you do

1. Use a plate or other flat, round object to trace a large circle on the fabric.
2. Cut out your circle of fabric.
3. Use scissors or a hole puncher to snip evenly spaced small holes around the circle of fabric, about 1 or 2 inches from the edge.
4. Thread your string or ribbon in and out through the holes.
5. Pull the string tight. You have a pouch!

# About the Author and Illustrator

**Gabriella Aldeman** (she/her) is a Panamanian American author who is constantly trying to mend her children's torn pants, broken toys, and stained everythings—nothing some colorful patches (or superglue) can't fix! She writes picture books in hopes that more children become readers and that all readers feel seen. She is also a professional translator and holds degrees from Georgetown University and the College of William and Mary. Gabriella lives in Fairfax, Virginia, with her partner and two children. This is her debut picture book. Please visit her at writebetween.com.

**Rocio Arreola Mendoza** (she/her) is a self-taught illustrator with a background in graphic design. She loves connecting with other creatives, and has worked with local colleagues to develop conferences, workshops, and drawing events in her city, including the activist-art centered Curcumas Creative Studio. You can find Rocío working in her home studio in Matamoros, Tamaulipas, in the high north of México, between the river and the sea. There she will be brewing Chinese tea, playing in the garden with her husband and son, and listening to folk music.